TO: Marcello, Aliana, Giovana

Frank 2018

for Papa Dan and Grandpa Henry

Pigs and Pens.

Frank Henry and the Zooband Band Copyright© 2015 by Frank Kamish and Paul Kamish and David Kamish.
Published in the United States by Pigs and Pens Publishing, Minneapolis, Minnesota USA

www.pigsandpens.com/magicalzoobands

Library of Congress Cataloging-in-Publication Data:
Kamish, Frank.
Frank Henry and the Zooband Band / by Frank, Paul and David Kamish
p.cm. - SUMMARY: Frank Henry and the Zooband Band help to harmonize the animals at the zoo
with the power of listening, music and Magical Zoobands.
Magical Zoobands are headbands with ears that give the lucky wearer a fresh set of ears for listening.

Library of Congress Control Number: 2015952943

ISBN 978-0-9968418-0-1

[1.Listening-Fiction 2. Music-Fiction 3. Communication- Fiction.]
Printed in the United States of America October 2015 10 9 8 7 6 5 4 3 2 1

Magical Zoobands is a registered trademark of Pigs and Pens Publishing

Frank Henry
and The ZooBand Band

BY
Frank Henry
Paul and David Kamish

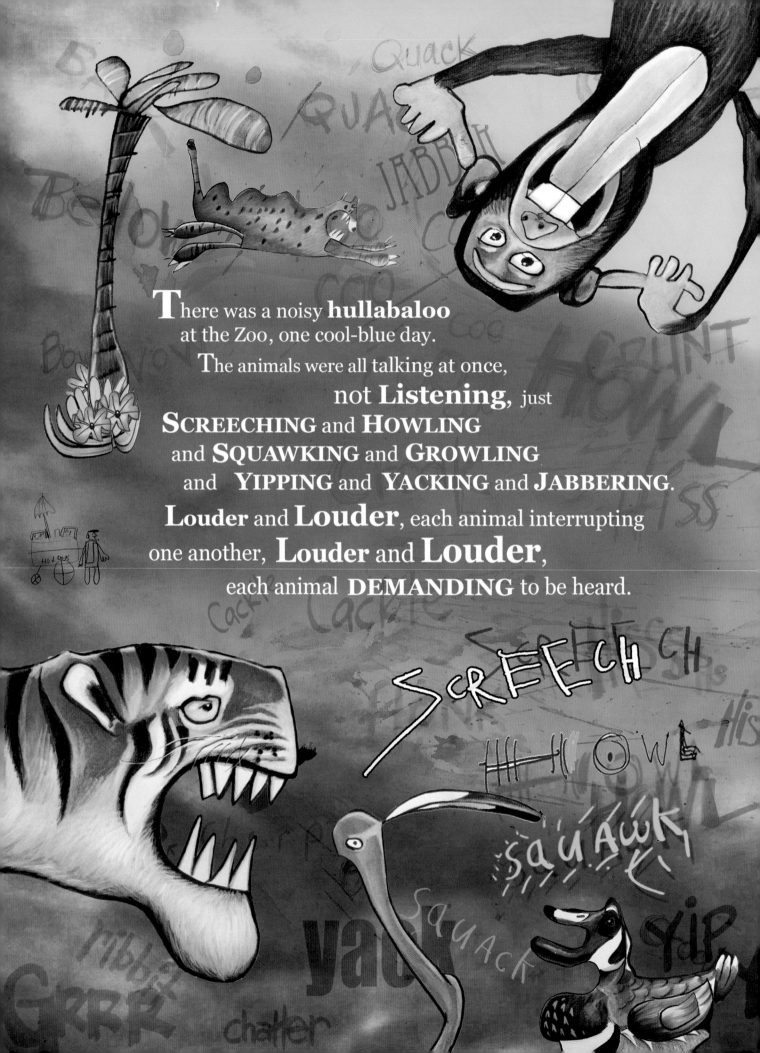

There was a noisy **hullabaloo**
at the Zoo, one cool-blue day.
The animals were all talking at once,
not **Listening**, just
SCREECHING and **HOWLING**
and **SQUAWKING** and **GROWLING**
and **YIPPING** and **YACKING** and **JABBERING**.
Louder and **Louder**, each animal interrupting
one another, **Louder** and **Louder**,
each animal **DEMANDING** to be heard.

To make matters worse, the music had stopped playing over the loud speakers. Everything at the Zoo, that quarrelsome day, was out of rhythm and off key.

MEANWHILE...

Need your help ASAP

. . . on the other side of town, **Frank Henry** and **the Zooband Band** were jammin' on a *jazzy* new song, when an urgent message came in from their old pals **Buster** and **Chipper Dipper**:

"Need your help ASAP. The animals are at it again."

Frank Henry's Great-Great-Great-Great Grandfather and
Buster's Great-Great-Great-Great Grandfather were great friends
long ago.

Frank Henry and the Zooband Band are called on in these situations when **Listening Powers** are needed. Frank Henry grabs the *Magical Zooband Horn* and they are *off to the rescue!*

Get your ears on!

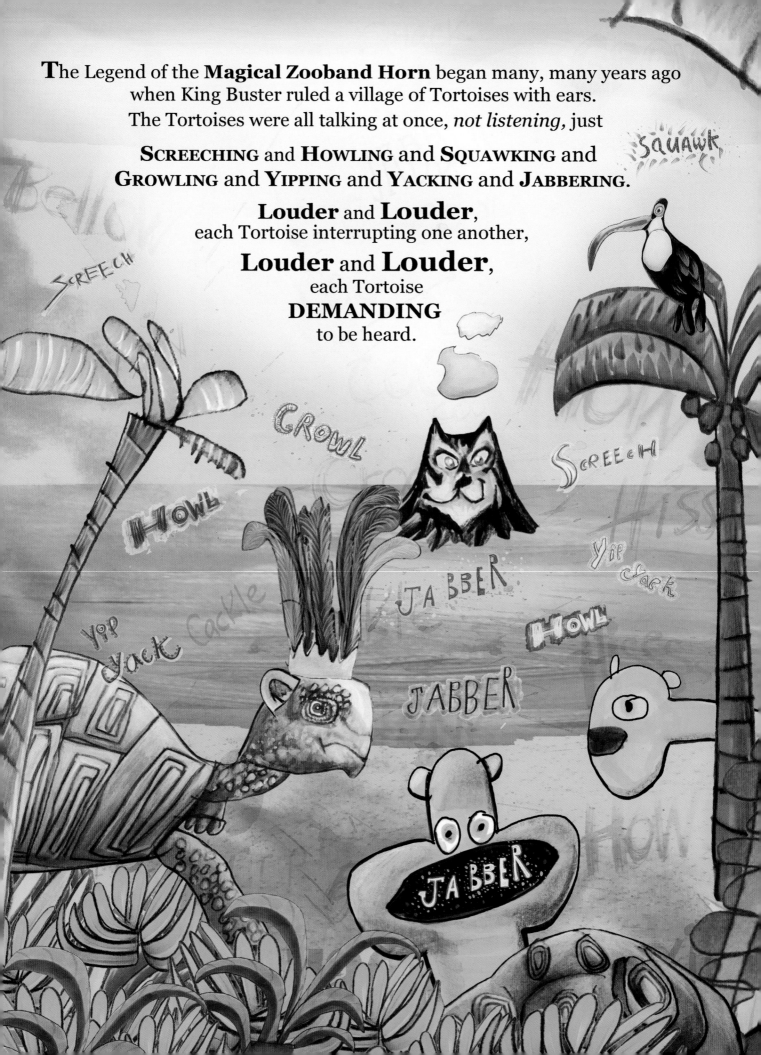

The Legend of the **Magical Zooband Horn** began many, many years ago when King Buster ruled a village of Tortoises with ears. The Tortoises were all talking at once, *not listening*, just

SCREECHING and **HOWLING** and **SQUAWKING** and **GROWLING** and **YIPPING** and **YACKING** and **JABBERING.**

Louder and **Louder**, each Tortoise interrupting one another, **Louder** and **Louder**, each Tortoise **DEMANDING** to be heard.

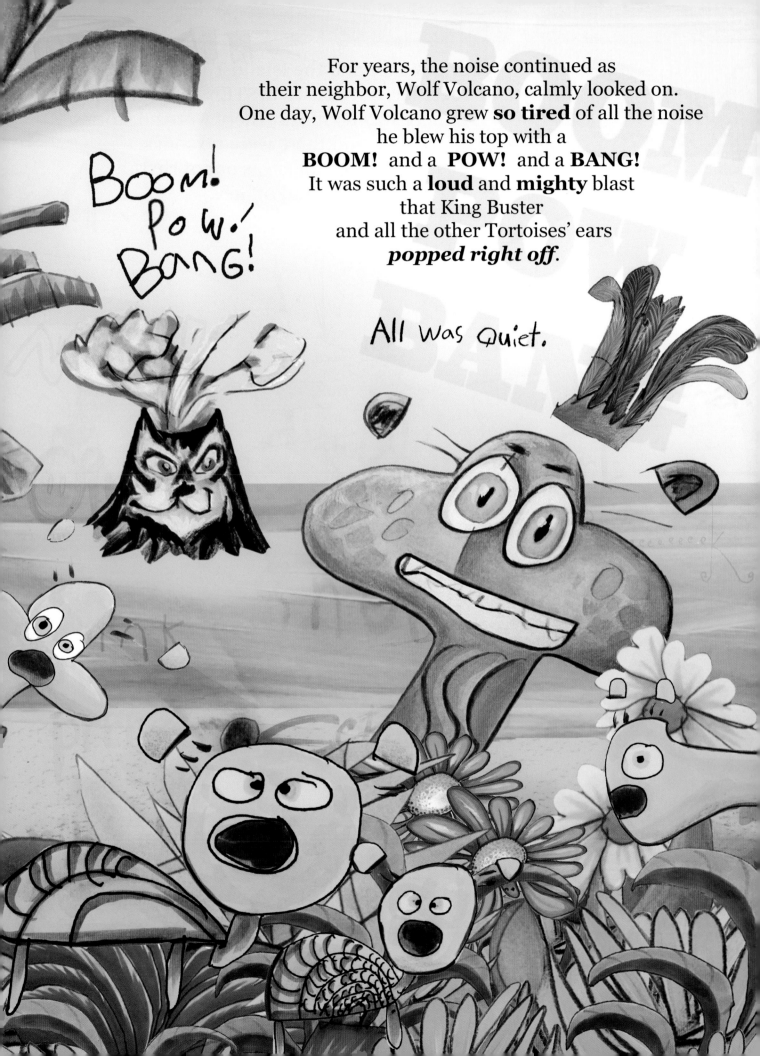

King Buster and the Island Tortoises now lived
together, not able to LISTEN to one another.
There was no music, there were no stories
and there were no songs.
Everything was out of rhythm
and off key.

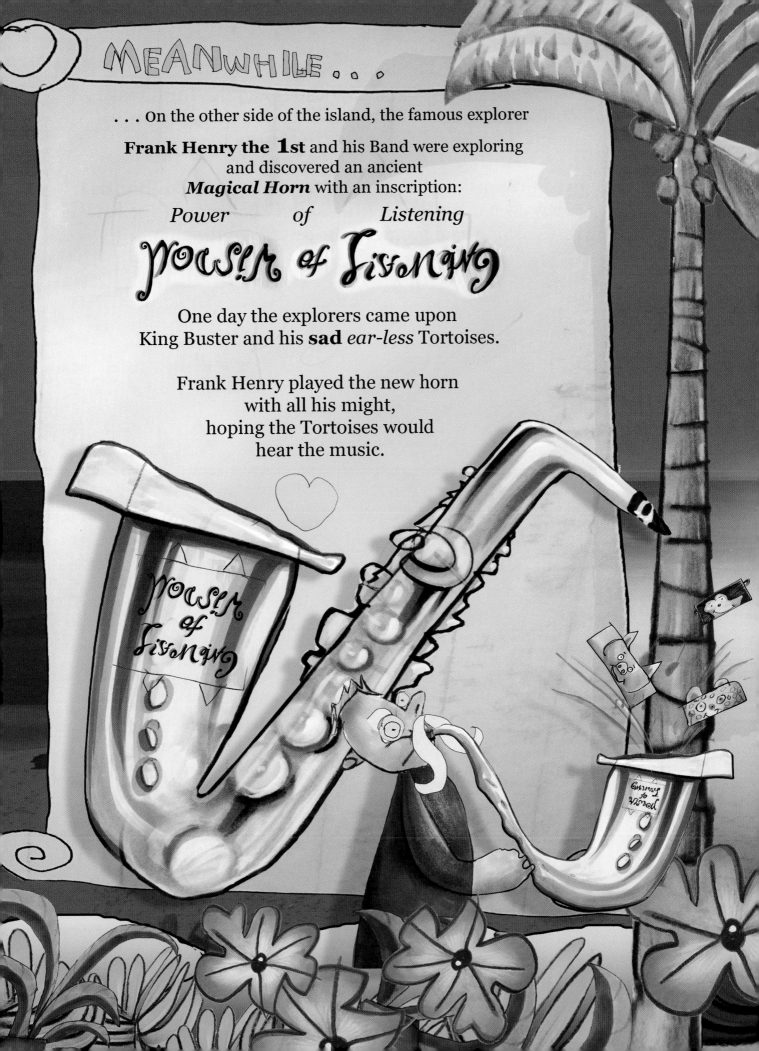

MEANWHILE . . .

. . . On the other side of the island, the famous explorer

Frank Henry the 1st and his Band were exploring
and discovered an ancient
Magical Horn with an inscription:

Power   of   Listening

One day the explorers came upon
King Buster and his **sad** *ear-less* Tortoises.

Frank Henry played the new horn
with all his might,
hoping the Tortoises would
hear the music.

Suddenly, headbands *with ears* flew from the horn,
soared high into the air
and landed *right-smack-dab* on the heads of all the Tortoises.
Magical Zoobands give the lucky wearer a ***fresh set of ears***,
not just for **hearing**, but for **listening** too.

They all enjoyed the music and decorated their **Magical Zoobands**.
They even made a ***volcano-sized*** Zooband
for Wolf Volcano using some of the sails from the ship.

Wolf Volcano **Loved** it !

Now they all listened to new stories, shared new ideas,
laughed at new jokes and sang new songs.

All was Peaceful.

Now, Back to
the Rescue!

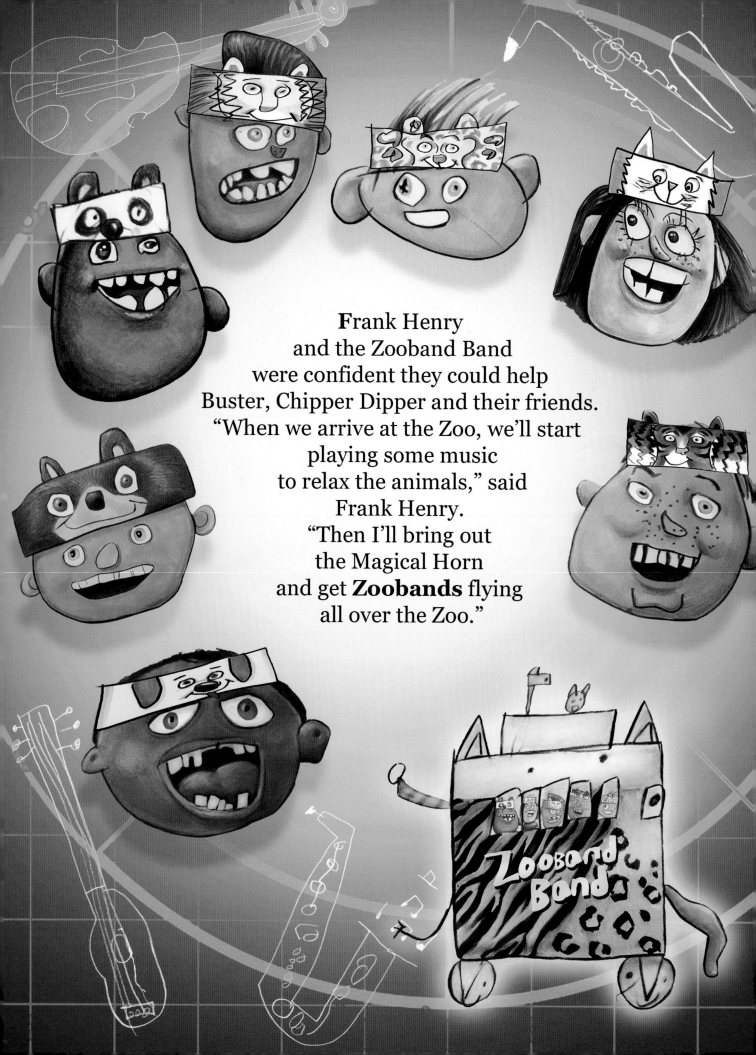

Frank Henry
and the Zooband Band
were confident they could help
Buster, Chipper Dipper and their friends.
"When we arrive at the Zoo, we'll start
playing some music
to relax the animals," said
Frank Henry.
"Then I'll bring out
the Magical Horn
and get **Zoobands** flying
all over the Zoo."

As the Zooband Band began to play the music,
the *curious* animals **stopped**
SCREEECHING and **HOWLING** and
SQUAWKING and **GROWLING** and
YIPPING and **YACKING**
and **JABBERING.**

Frank Henry
BLEW the Magical Zooband Horn
with all his might.

Magical Zoobands flew high into the sky
and floated down *right-smack-dab* on the animals' heads.
Suddenly . . . with a ***fresh set of ears*** . . .

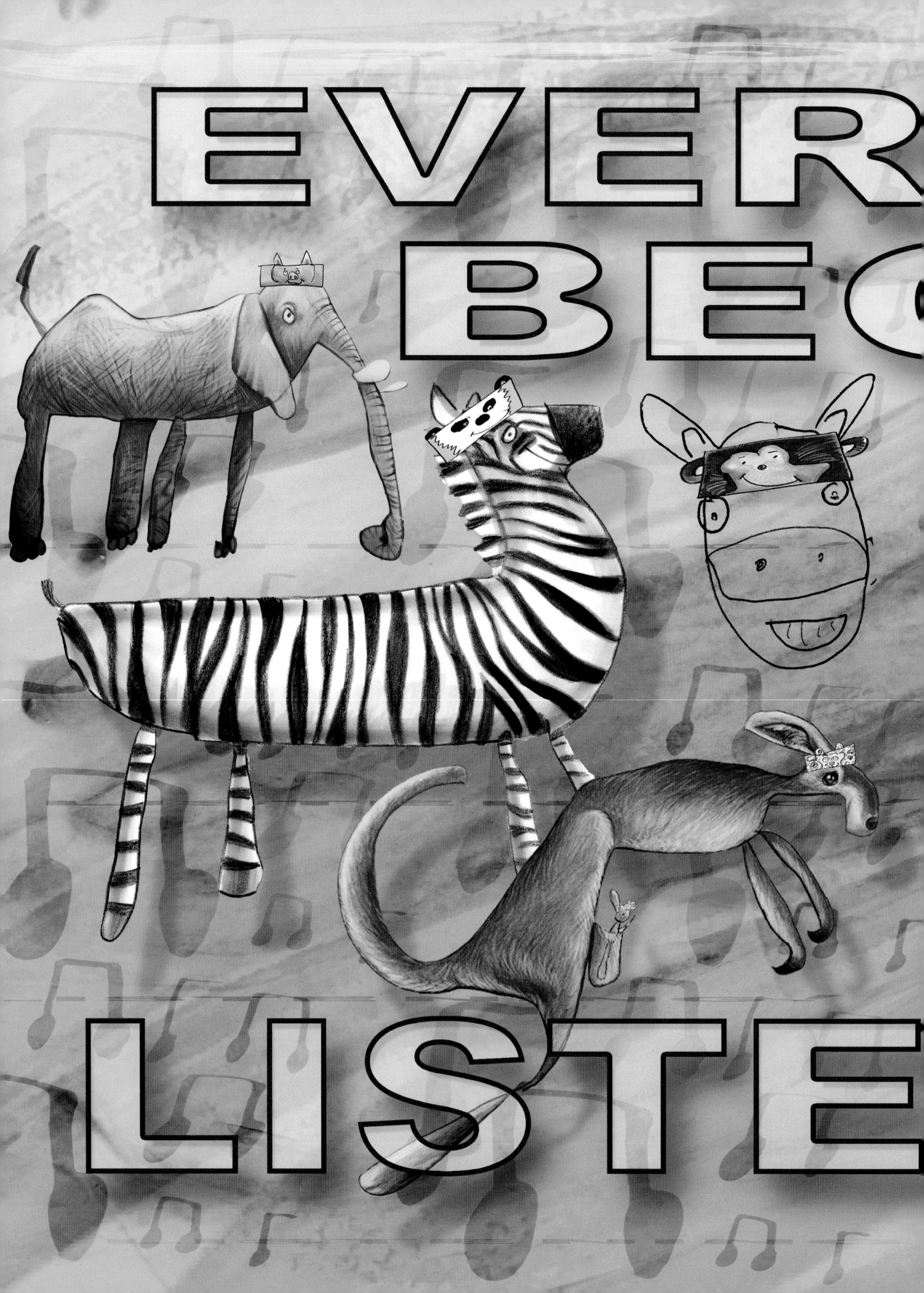
EVER
BE
LISTE

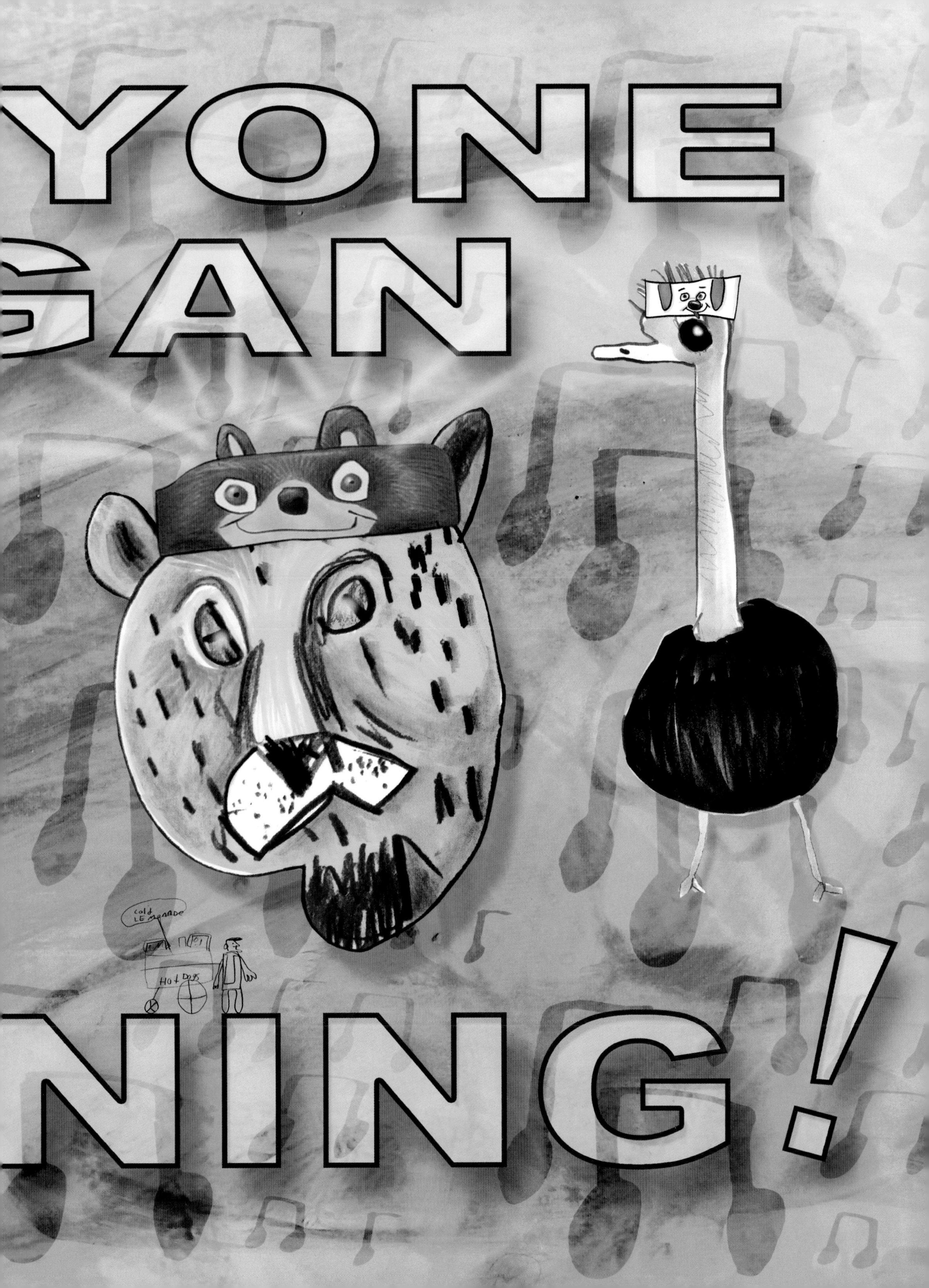
YONE
GAN
Cold LEMonADE
Hot Dogs
NING!

. . . and understanding and learning.

Now they listened to **new stories**, shared **new ideas**, laughed at **new jokes** and sang **new songs**. All Was Peaceful.

Sometimes all you need is a ***fresh set of ears.***
The **Magical Zoobands** had brought
peace and harmony back to the Zoo.

Buster, Chipper Dipper and all the animals waved good-bye as
Frank Henry and the Zooband Band
headed for home!

. . . and this is the end of the story, *tralla, tralla, tralla.*

Thanks for reading our book.

Check out our website:
- Fun art ideas
- Creative projects
- Design your own
  Magical Zoobands and more

www.PigsandPens.com

Frank Henry
Paul and David Kamish

Pigs and Pens